Team Spirit

THE PHOENIX SUNS

BY

MARK STEWART

Content Consultant
Matt Zeysing
Historian and Archivist
The Naismith Memorial Basketball Hall of Fame

NORWOOD HOUSE PRESS

CHICAGO, ILLINOIS

Norwood House Press
P.O. Box 316598
Chicago, Illinois 60631

For information regarding Norwood House Press, please visit our website at:
www.norwoodhousepress.com or call 866-565-2900.

Editor: Mike Kennedy
Designer: Ron Jaffe
Project Management: Black Book Partners, LLC.

Special thanks to: Kathleen Baxter and Amanda Jones.

Library of Congress Cataloging-in-Publication Data

Stewart, Mark.
   The Phoenix Suns / by Mark Stewart ; with content consultant Matt
Zeysing.
       p. cm. -- (Team spirit)
   Summary: "Presents the history, accomplishments and key personalities of
the Phoenix Suns basketball team. Includes timelines, quotes,maps,glossary
and websites to visit"--Provided by publisher.
   Includes bibliographical references and index.
   ISBN-13: 978-1-59953-010-9 (alk. paper)
   ISBN-10: 1-59953-010-4 (alk. paper)
   1. Phoenix Suns (Basketball team)--History--Juvenile literature. I. Zeysing,
Matt. II. Title. III. Series.
   GV885.52.P47S74 2006
   796.323'640979173--dc22
                                                             2005029908

Manufactured in the United States of America.

COVER PHOTO: The Phoenix Suns celebrate a victory in 2004.

Table of Contents

CHAPTER	PAGE
Meet the Suns	4
Way Back When	6
The Team Today	10
Home Court	12
Dressed For Success	14
We Won!	16
Go-To Guys	20
On the Sidelines	24
One Great Day	26
Legend Has It	28
It Really Happened	30
Team Spirit	32
Timeline	34
Fun Facts	36
Talking Hoops	38
For the Record	40
Pinpoints	42
Play Ball	44
Glossary	46
Places to Go	47
Index	48

SPORTS WORDS & VOCABULARY WORDS: In this book, you will find many words that are new to you. You may also see familiar words used in new ways. The glossary on page 46 gives the meanings of basketball words, as well as "everyday" words that have special basketball meanings. These words appear in **bold type** throughout the book. The glossary on page 47 gives the meanings of vocabulary words that are not related to basketball. They appear in ***bold italic type*** throughout the book.

BASKETBALL SEASONS: Because each basketball season begins late in one year and ends early in the next, seasons are not named after years. Instead, they are written out as two years separated by a dash, for example 1944–45 or 2005–06.

Meet the Suns

There are many ways to win a basketball game. A team can earn a victory with great shooting, or with smart defense. Some nights it takes perfect passing to outplay an opponent, while other nights the game is won **in the paint** with tough rebounding. Like most teams, the Phoenix Suns have used each of these ingredients in their winning recipe.

What sets the Suns apart is that they have always built their team around one *extraordinary* player—a star who understands the importance of teamwork, but who also knows how to take charge...and take your breath away.

This book tells the story of the Suns. They began as a basketball experiment. Now they are a success. When you watch the Suns play, you can count on two things: You will see basketball at its best, and someone, sometime, will do something that makes you say "Wow!"

Bo Outlaw hugs Steve Nash as the Suns wait for the
final buzzer to sound during a victory in the 2005 playoffs.

Way Back When

GAIL GOODRICH
guard

PHOENIX

Who will watch basketball in the desert? This was what the sports world was wondering in 1968, when the **National Basketball Association (NBA)** announced that it was adding a new team in Phoenix, Arizona. A man named Richard Bloch thought that the state deserved a big-time sports team. He believed that the people of Arizona would support one. Bloch and his partners bought the new team, which they named the Phoenix Suns.

In their first season, the Suns were made up of little-known players selected from other NBA teams. The *general manager*, Jerry Colangelo, chose very wisely. He took Gail Goodrich from the Los Angeles Lakers and Dick Van Arsdale from the New York Knicks. They had been substitutes on their old teams. With the Suns, they became stars. Colangelo would later coach the Suns, and eventually become the team's owner.

ABOVE: Gail Goodrich, the Suns' first great player. **RIGHT**: Connie Hawkins got his first chance to play in the NBA with the Suns.

In their second season, the Suns added Connie Hawkins to their lineup. Hawkins was a legend from the playgrounds of New York City. He had been unfairly **banned** from the league many years earlier. This was his first chance to show his skills against the best players in basketball. In 1969–70—his first NBA season—Hawkins led the Suns to the **playoffs**. The city of Phoenix went wild. Everyone was talking about the Suns. The fans who came to see them play at Veterans' Memorial Coliseum were so loud that the arena was nicknamed the "Madhouse on McDowell."

Many more talented players would wear the Suns uniform over the next few years, including Paul Silas, Charlie Scott, Paul Westphal, and Alvan Adams. In 1976, the Suns made it to the **NBA Finals**. They were defeated by the mighty Boston Celtics in a thrilling series.

The Suns won a lot of games during the 1980s. They were led by stars like Walter Davis, Larry Nance, Kevin Johnson, and Tom Chambers. But they did not make it back to the NBA Finals until 1993. The star of this team was Charles Barkley. He taught his teammates that winning took hard work, but could also be fun. Barkley and the Suns nearly beat Michael Jordan and the Chicago Bulls in the 1993 finals.

Charles Barkley tries to distract Michael Jordan during the 1993 NBA Finals.

The Team Today

In recent years, some of the most *dynamic* players in the NBA have worn the Suns' uniform. Jason Kidd, Stephon Marbury, Shawn Marion, Amare Stoudemire, and Steve Nash have continued the team's *tradition* of exciting play and winning basketball.

These smart, talented stars have helped the team win despite the fact that Phoenix has not had a typical NBA center. Without a big man in the middle, the Suns have to be faster on offense and quicker on defense. They are very good at creating **mismatches**, which give the team an advantage for a few seconds. What they do with those few seconds often means the difference between winning and losing.

The Suns play a fearless style of basketball. They race up and down the court past exhausted opponents, and score a lot of points on thunderous slam-dunks and *majestic* three-pointers. When the Suns are ahead, they never let up. When they are behind, they never give in. You cannot relax when you are playing against the Suns, and you can never count them out.

Amare Stoudemire shows the focus that made him one of the NBA's top stars.

Home Court

The Suns play their home games in America West Arena, which is located in downtown Phoenix. It opened in 1992, and is one of the most popular arenas among NBA players, who once voted it best in the league. The fans like the arena, too. There are no "bad" seats, and a gigantic four-sided scoreboard is easy to see. The Suns often put on fantastic laser light shows.

The Suns are very hard to beat at home. When the building is full of fans, it is extremely loud. This makes it difficult for visiting players to concentrate. Phoenix players like all the noise. It gives them more energy and makes it easier to *overwhelm* their opponents.

AMERICA WEST ARENA BY THE NUMBERS

- *America West Arena holds 18,422 people for basketball games.*
- *In 1995, the NBA played its annual All-Star Game in the Suns' arena.*
- *In 1998, the WNBA Finals were held there.*
- *Many NBA teams have used the Suns' home as a model when building their own arenas.*
- *The Suns beat the Los Angeles Clippers 111–105 in the first game at America West Arena.*

The gigantic four-sided scoreboard in the Suns' arena means fans never miss a moment of the action.

Dressed for Success

For 25 years, the Suns' uniform featured rising suns on each leg of the shorts. The team colors were red, white and blue-purple. In 1992, the team redesigned its uniform. Purple and orange became more important colors, and the jerseys featured a modern-looking sun. When the Suns played at home, in their white uniforms, the sun looked like it was rising. When the Suns were on the road, in their purple uniforms, the sun appeared to be setting.

In recent years, the Suns have gone "back to basics." Sometimes they wear a uniform that looks a lot like their original one. Often they wear a jersey with the letters PHX, which is short for Phoenix. Their basic home uniform is white with purple sides and SUNS written across the front. Their basic road uniform is purple with gray sides and PHOENIX on the front. On both uniforms, a player's number is surrounded by an oval that looks like a planet's orbit.

Mel Counts models the Suns' uniform from the 1971–72 season.

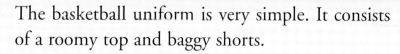

UNIFORM BASICS

The basketball uniform is very simple. It consists of a roomy top and baggy shorts.

- The top hangs from the shoulders, with big "scoops" for the arms and neck. This style has not changed much over the years.

- Shorts, however, have changed a lot. They used to be very short, so players could move their legs freely. In the last 20 years, shorts have actually gotten longer and much baggier.

Basketball uniforms look the same as they did long ago...until you look very closely. In the old days, the shorts had belts and buckles. The tops were made of a thick cotton called "jersey," which got very heavy when players sweated. Later, uniforms were made of shiny **satin**. They may have looked great, but they did not "breathe." Players got very hot! Today, most uniforms are made of **synthetic** materials that soak up sweat and keep the body cool.

Steve Nash in the Suns' home uniform.

We Won!

Winning 50 games says a lot about an NBA team. It means they have a lot of talent, a good coach, and they play hard every night. Since 1979, the Suns have reached 50 wins in more than half of their seasons. Only one other team—the Los Angeles Lakers—can match this record.

The Suns have won the **Western Conference** and made it to the NBA Finals twice, in 1976 and 1993. Although they did not win the league championship in those years, the team had a lot to be proud of.

In 1976, the Suns played the Golden State Warriors to decide who was "the best in the west." The Warriors were the league's 1975 champions. No one thought Phoenix had a chance, but the Suns won four games to three.

The Suns played great team defense against the Warriors in the 1976 playoffs.

Coach John McLeod hugs Curtis Perry as the Suns celebrate their victory over the Warriors in the 1976 Western Conference finals.

In 1993, Charles Barkley, the league's **Most Valuable Player (MVP)**, led the Suns back to the Western Conference Finals. They had quite a battle with the **deep** and talented Seattle Supersonics. With the series tied at two games each, the Suns needed to win their last two games at home. With the help of their home crowd, they did.

The Suns did not reach the Western Conference Finals again until 2005. They missed a chance to return to the NBA Finals when they lost a hard-fought series to the San Antonio Spurs. Phoenix fans were disappointed that they came so close. They know how much fun it is to root for their team in the NBA Finals. However, they also know how lucky they are to cheer for a team like the Suns--the kind of team that has a chance to win it all every year.

LEFT: Charles Barkley puts in a lay-up during the 1993 Western Conference Finals. **ABOVE**: Charles Barkley and Danny Ainge show the competitive fire of the 1993 Suns.

Go-To Guys

To be a true star in the NBA, you need more than a great shot. You have to be a "go-to guy"—someone teammates trust to make the winning play when the seconds are ticking away in a big game. Phoenix fans have had a lot to cheer about over the years, including these great stars...

THE PIONEERS

GAIL GOODRICH 6' 1" Guard

- BORN: 4/23/1943 • PLAYED FOR TEAM: 1968–69 TO 1969–70

When Gail Goodrich decided he wanted to score, there was no way to guard him. One way or another, he was going to get his shot. Goodrich was the Suns' first great player, and the first player to wear a Phoenix uniform in the NBA **All-Star Game**. He was elected to the **Hall of Fame** in 1996.

DICK VAN ARSDALE 6' 5" Guard

- BORN: 2/22/1943
- PLAYED FOR TEAM: 1968–69 TO 1976–77

Dick Van Arsdale played for the team so long that he was called the "Original Sun." He had an identical twin, Tom, who joined him on the Suns for the 1976–77 season. The brothers retired after playing together for one year.

ABOVE: The Van Arsdale twins—Tom and Dick.
TOP RIGHT: Connie Hawkins **BOTTOM RIGHT**: Paul Westphal

CONNIE HAWKINS   6' 8" Forward

• BORN: 7/17/1942 • PLAYED FOR TEAM: 1969–70 TO 1973–74

Connie Hawkins gave the Suns real star power. He was the most athletic and exciting forward in the NBA from the first day he stepped on the court. The high-flying "Hawk" would swoop in on the basket for amazing dunks and rebounds.

ALVAN ADAMS   6' 9" Center/Forward

• BORN: 7/19/1954 • PLAYED FOR TEAM: 1975–76 TO 1987–88

Alvan Adams was not as big or as strong as the centers he guarded, but he could do a lot of things they could not—like dribble, pass, run, and shoot from the outside. He was **Rookie of the Year** in 1976 and played his entire career with the Suns.

PAUL WESTPHAL   6' 4" Guard

• BORN: 11/30/1950 • PLAYED FOR TEAM: 1975–76 TO 1979–80

When the Suns traded All-Star Charlie Scott for bench-warmer Paul Westphal after the 1974–75 season, the reaction of Phoenix fans was "Paul who?" One year later, he led the team to the NBA Finals. "Westy" **averaged** more than 20 points per game each year he played with the Suns.

WALTER DAVIS   6' 6" Guard/Forward

• BORN: 9/9/1954 • PLAYED FOR TEAM: 1977–78 TO 1987–88

Walter Davis's jumpshot was a thing of beauty. He was so smooth and sleek on the court that fans called him the "Greyhound." He scored 15,666 points—more than anyone else in team history.

MODERN STARS

KEVIN JOHNSON   6' 1" Guard

• BORN: 3/4/1966   • PLAYED FOR TEAM: 1987–88 TO 1999–00

Like so many Suns, Kevin Johnson could do many things well. He was a lightning-fast **ball-handler**, a great shooter, and an expert passer. He still holds the team's all-time record for **assists**.

DAN MAJERLE   6' 6" Guard/Forward

• BORN: 9/9/1965   • PLAYED FOR TEAM: 1988–89 TO 1994–95 AND 2001–02

Basketball comes easy for many players, but not for Dan Majerle. He worked hard every second he was on the court. Majerle (pronounced Mar-lee) was a good defender and excellent three-point shooter.

CHARLES BARKLEY   6' 6" Forward

• BORN: 2/20/1963

• PLAYED FOR TEAM: 1992–93 TO 1995–96

Charles Barkley had a big mouth and a big game— and the fans adored him. The Suns were already good when he joined them, and "Sir Charles" made them great. Barkley was short for an NBA power forward, but his wide body made him difficult to guard and impossible to **box out**.

TOP: Kevin Johnson   **ABOVE**: Charles Barkley
TOP RIGHT: Shawn Marion   **BOTTOM RIGHT**: Amare Stoudemire

SHAWN MARION 6' 7" Forward

• BORN: 5/7/1978 • FIRST SEASON WITH TEAM: 1999–00

When the Suns drafted Shawn Marion in the first round, they thought they could count on him for 20 points and 10 rebounds a game. Not only did he give the team these numbers, Marion quickly became an important team leader.

JASON KIDD 6' 4" Guard

• BORN: 3/23/1973 • PLAYED FOR TEAM: 1996–97 TO 2000–01

Jason Kidd was the master of the "no-look" pass. He would *lure* a defender one way with his eyes, then flick the ball to a wide-open teammate. Kidd was the first Sun ever to lead the NBA in assists.

STEVE NASH 6' 3" Guard

• BORN: 2/7/1974 • FIRST PLAYED FOR TEAM: 1996–97 TO 1997–98

• RETURNED TO TEAM: 2004–05

The Suns drafted Steve Nash in 1996, and then unwisely traded him two years later. When the scrappy point guard returned to Phoenix, he was named the NBA's Most Valuable Player for 2004–05.

AMARE STOUDEMIRE 6' 10" Forward

• BORN: 11/16/1982

• FIRST SEASON WITH TEAM: 2002–03

Amare Stoudemire may have joined the Suns as a teenager, but he was already "the man" when it came to *intimidating* opponents. The 2003 NBA Rookie of the Year helped Phoenix become a championship *contender* in just his third season.

On the Sidelines

A good NBA coach not only knows how to get the best out of his players, he knows how to get them to share the ball. This is not always easy, especially with so much talent on every team. The Suns have been very lucky over the years. They have had *unselfish* players, and excellent leaders on the sidelines to guide them.

The team's most popular coach was Cotton Fitzsimmons. He coached the Suns three different times. He was friendly and funny, but very serious about basketball. Fitzsimmons was on the sidelines when the Suns had their first winning season in 1970–71.

The first coach to take the Suns to the NBA Finals was John MacLeod. He encouraged his players to be creative, and to do the unexpected. The coach of the team when Phoenix reached the 1993 NBA Finals was Paul Westphal, the star of MacLeod's team.

The owner of the Suns, Jerry Colangelo, was once the team's coach. Colangelo actually started as the general manager. During the 1969–70 season, he took over the team. The Suns went 24–20 the rest of the way and made it to the playoffs for the first time.

Owner Jerry Colangelo congratulates Amare Stoudemire on his NBA Rookie of the Year award.

One Great Day

The city of Phoenix was buzzing when the 1993 NBA Finals began. The Suns had a chance to win a championship—if they could defeat the mighty Chicago Bulls. When the Suns lost the first two games, however, the experts thought the Bulls would sweep the series four games to none.

As the Suns took the floor for Game Three in Chicago, every man knew what they were playing for: pride. They also knew that their star, Charles Barkley, might have to play one-handed. He had injured his elbow and could barely move it.

Just when all looked lost, Kevin Johnson and Dan Majerle stepped into the spotlight. Johnson covered Michael Jordan like a blanket and slowly wore him down. Majerle hit one 3-pointer after another to keep the Suns close. At the end of four quarters, the score was tied 103–103. The Bulls looked nervous and the Suns looked loose. Barkley was smiling and patting his teammates on the back. The pain was gone and he was having a great game.

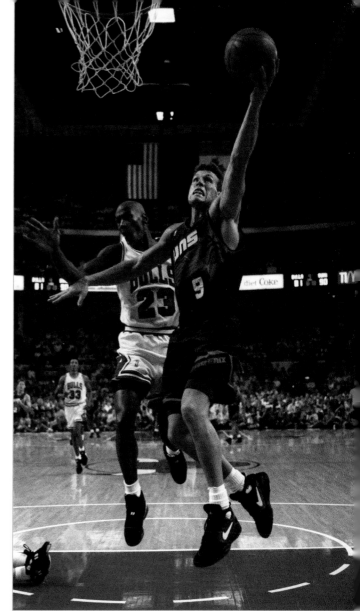

Dan Majerle scores on Michael Jordan during the 1993 NBA Finals.

In the extra period, Jordan tried to win the game, but he could not break free of Johnson's defense. The Suns had an answer for everything the Bulls did, and after two five-minute **overtimes** the score was still tied.

Phoenix finally triumphed in the third overtime. Majerle's sixth 3-pointer gave the Suns a slim lead, and then Barkley stole a pass and dunked to make the score 123–118. The Suns held on to win 129–121.

The Bulls were in shock after this loss. The Suns beat them again in Chicago, and almost won the championship. Only an amazing last-second shot by John Paxson enabled the Bulls to capture their third straight title. Had Paxson missed that shot, Phoenix fans have no doubt that the 1993 NBA championship banner would be hanging in their home arena today.

Legend Has It

How did the Suns discover their mascot, the Gorilla?

LEGEND HAS IT that he first appeared at a Suns game to deliver a singing telegram. Bob Woolf, the man behind the mask, got such a big cheer from the crowd that the Suns hired him to be their full-time mascot. In 2005—25 years after his first appearance—the Gorilla was *inducted* into the Mascot Hall of Fame.

Charles Barkley "goes ape" for the Phoenix Gorilla.

How did the Suns get their name?

LEGEND HAS IT that it was one of 28,000 names mailed to the *Arizona Republic* during a contest held by the newspaper in 1968. A woman named Selinda King entered the winning name, and received **season tickets** and a $1,000 prize. Among the losing names were Prickly Pears, Arizoniacs, Desert Rats, Jumping Beans, and Sweethearts.

Who hit the most amazing shot in Suns history?

LEGEND HAS IT that it was Garfield Heard. He made the shot against the Boston Celtics in Game Five of the 1976 NBA Finals. The series was tied, and the teams were in double-overtime. Boston led by two points with one second left on the clock. Heard received a pass more than 20 feet from the basket, and in one motion spun around and heaved the ball into the air. It went right in the hoop, forcing a third overtime period. The Celtics ended up winning the game 128–126, and went on to win the series. Still, Heard's **clutch shot** will always be remembered as the greatest in team history.

It Really Happened

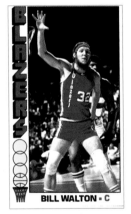

Bill Walton

Anything can happen in basketball, including rainouts. This has happened to the Suns not once, but twice! The first time a Suns game was washed out was in the fall of 1974. The Suns were supposed to play the Portland Trailblazers in a **pre-season game**. Phoenix fans ignored the powerful thunderstorms that day and headed to Veterans' Memorial Coliseum, the old arena the Suns called home from 1968 to 1992. They wanted to see the NBA's new rookie *sensation*, Bill Walton.

As the fans settled into their seats, they noticed a slow, steady drip from the coliseum ceiling. The roof had sprung a leak and water was splashing onto the court. The Suns were worried that players might slip and injure themselves. When they announced that the game was cancelled, the fans were angry. The team gave fans free tickets to two other games, and the smiles returned to their faces.

Twelve years later, in 1986, it was Seattle fans who were angry. The Suns were playing the Supersonics in the Seattle Center Coliseum during another violent storm. Sure enough, the roof sprung a leak and a puddle began to form at center court. At first,

Veterans' Memorial Coliseum in Phoenix. In 2005, the arena was used to house victims of Hurricane Katrina.

the teams agreed to play around the wet spot. Many fans jokingly opened their umbrellas. But as the puddle grew in the second quarter, it was no longer funny. For the first time in pro basketball history, a regular-season game was called off due to rain. The leak was fixed the next day and the game continued. The Suns got the last laugh when they won 117–114.

Team Spirit

Suns fans are very smart when it comes to basketball. They understand how a good team is built, and they can tell the difference between a team player and a selfish one. They also cheer just as loud for their **role players** and substitutes as they do for their big-name stars.

Back in 1968, the experts doubted that Phoenix would support an NBA team. The city proved the experts wrong. In the Suns' first season, crowds of 5,000 or more would show up to root for the team. Since then, the team has become more and more popular each season. Today, the Suns' arena is packed every night, with crowds of more than 17,000 cheering for the team. During the playoffs, Phoenix fans have been known to do all sorts of crazy things for a chance to buy a ticket.

The players love the Phoenix fans. When the team is winning, the Suns' arena is an amazing place to play. When they are behind, everyone pulls together. That is what makes being a Sun—and playing in Phoenix—one of the best jobs in basketball.

Suns players like Steve Nash lead the cheers when they are not in the game.

Timeline

The basketball season is played from October through June. That means each season takes place at the end of one year and the beginning of the next. In this timeline, the accomplishments of the Suns are shown by season.

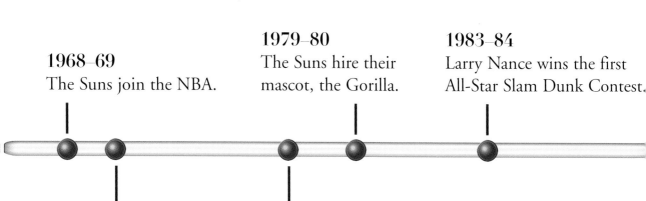

1968–69
The Suns join the NBA.

1979–80
The Suns hire their mascot, the Gorilla.

1983–84
Larry Nance wins the first All-Star Slam Dunk Contest.

1969–70
The Suns make the playoffs for the first time, and nearly **upset** the Los Angeles Lakers.

1975–76
The Suns reach the NBA Finals for the first time.

PHOENIX SUNS

Charles
Barkley

Amare
Stoudemire

1992–93
MVP Charles Barkley leads
the Suns to NBA Finals.

2002–03
Amare Stoudemire is named
NBA Rookie of the Year.

1986–87
Jerry Colangelo
leads a group that
buys the Suns for
$44.5 million.

1994–95
The Suns win 50-
plus games for the
seventh year in a row.

2004–05
Steve Nash wins
the MVP award.

Steve
Nash

Fun Facts

MUSIC TO THEIR EARS!

The Suns' original ownership group included singer Andy Williams and musician Henry Mancini. They performed a concert together after the team's first home game in 1968.

HOT SHOT

Connie Hawkins played for the Harlem Globetrotters before he joined the Suns.

WE MEANT TO SAY TAILS

Before the NBA draft in 1969, the Suns lost a coin flip with the Milwaukee Bucks. Had they won, they would have selected future Hall of Famer Kareem Abdul-Jabbar.

WHAT A BARGAIN

Stan Fabe, the man who designed the team's original *logo*, charged just $200 for his work.

KICK BALL!

Steve Nash's father was a top **professional** soccer player in Europe.

WIN SOME, LOSE SOME

In 1997, the Suns became the first NBA team to win at least 10 in a row and lose at least 10 in a row in the same season.

JAM SESSION

The Suns have had two players win the NBA's Slam Dunk Contest. The first was Larry Nance in 1984. The second was Cedric Ceballos in 1992. Ceballos called his winning dunk "Hocus Pocus." He did it blindfolded.

LIKE FATHER, LIKE SON

Jerry Colangelo was named the NBA's top *executive* four times during the 1970s, 1980s, and 1990. In 2005, his son, Bryan, won the award.

LEFT: Kareem Abdul-Jabbar
RIGHT: Cedric Ceballos

Talking Hoops

DICK VAN ARSDALE • F

Dick Van Arsdale

"I wouldn't trade that for being head of a major corporation or President of the United States, because I wanted to be a ballplayer."

—Dick Van Arsdale, on playing in the NBA for the Suns

"I remember the first time I landed here, I was trying to make an impression and I had on a suit and a shirt and a tie and I heard the pilot say, 'Good Evening, we're landing in Phoenix, the temperature is 117!'"

—Connie Hawkins, on his first trip to Phoenix

"I always feel like I have something to prove. No one ever expected me to be here, so that feeling of being an underdog is **ingrained** in me."

—Steve Nash, on why he plays so hard

"The only difference between a good shot and a bad shot is if it goes in or not."

—Charles Barkley, on the art of shooting

"Our fans are some of the best in the NBA."

—Announcer Al McCoy, on Phoenix fans

"I'm just a big, fun-loving guy who's only mean on the basketball court."

—Amare Stoudemire, on his style of play

"I'd just like to thank the fans. They've really supported me and been behind me 100 percent...I felt like that's what I gave them every time I went on the floor."

—Dan Majerle, on Phoenix fans

Al McCoy, the "voice" of the Suns.

For the Record

T he great Suns teams and players have left their marks on the record books. These are the "best of the best"…

Alvan Adams

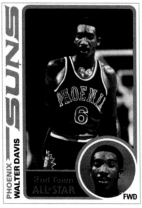

Walter Davis

SUNS AWARD WINNERS

WINNER	AWARD	SEASON
Alvan Adams	Rookie of the Year	1975–76
Walter Davis	Rookie of the Year	1977–78
Larry Nance	Slam Dunk Champion	1983–84
Eddie Johnson	Sixth Man Award*	1988–89
Cotton Fitzsimmons	Coach of the Year	1988–89
Cedric Ceballos	Slam Dunk Champion	1991–92
Charles Barkley	NBA MVP	1992–93
Danny Manning	Sixth Man Award	1998–99
Rodney Rodgers	Sixth Man Award	1999–00
Amare Stoudemire	Rookie of the Year	2002–03
Steve Nash	NBA MVP	2004–05

The award given each year to the NBA's best substitute

SUNS ACHIEVEMENTS

ACHIEVEMENT	SEASON
Western Conference Champions	1975–76
Pacific Division Champions	1980–81
Pacific Division Champions	1992–93
Western Conference Champions	1992–93
Pacific Division Champions	1994–95
Pacific Division Champions	2004–05

Charles Barkley

Cotton Fitzsimmons

Pinpoints

The history of a basketball team is made up of many smaller stories. These stories take place all over the map—not just in the city a team calls "home." Match the push-pins on these maps to the Team Facts and you will begin to see the story of the Suns unfold!

TEAM FACTS

1   Phoenix, Arizona—*The Suns have played here since 1968.*

2   Sacramento, California—*Kevin Johnson was born here.*

3   Torrance, California—*Paul Westphal was born here.*

4   Ogden, Utah—*Tom Chambers was born here.*

5   Chicago, Illinois—*Shawn Marion was born here.*

6   Indianapolis, Indiana—*Dick Van Arsdale was born here.*

7   Boston, Massachusetts—*The Suns and Celtics played a triple-overtime game in the 1976 NBA Finals here.*

8   New York City, New York—*Connie Hawkins was born here.*

9   Pineville, North Carolina—*Walter Davis was born here.*

10   Leeds, Alabama—*Charles Barkley was born here.*

11   Lake Wells, Florida—*Amare Stoudemire was born here.*

12   Johannesburg, South Africa—*Steve Nash was born here.*

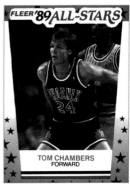

Tom Chambers

Play Ball

Basketball is a sport played by two teams of five players. NBA games have four 12-minute quarters—48 minutes in all—and the team that scores the most points when time has run out is the winner. Most baskets count for two points. Players who make shots from beyond the three-point line receive an extra point. Baskets made from the free-throw line count for one point. Free throws are penalty shots awarded to a team, usually after an opponent has committed a foul. A foul is called when one player makes hard contact with another.

Players can move around all they want, but the player with the ball cannot. He must bounce the ball with one hand or the other (but never both) in order to go from one part of the court to another. As long as he keeps "dribbling," he can keep moving.

In the NBA, teams must attempt a shot every 24 seconds, so there is little time to waste. The job of the defense is to make it as difficult as possible to take a good shot—and to grab the ball if the other team shoots and misses.

This may sound simple, but anyone who has played the game knows that basketball can be very complicated. Every player on the court has a job to do. Different players have different strengths and weaknesses. The coach must mix these players in just the right way, and teach them to work together as one.

The more you play and watch basketball, the more "little things" you are likely to notice. The next time you are at a game, look for these plays:

PLAY LIST

ALLEY-OOP—A play where the passer throws the ball just to the side of the rim—so a teammate can catch it and dunk in one motion.

BACK-DOOR PLAY—A play where the passer waits for his teammate to fake the defender away from the basket—then throws him the ball when he cuts back toward the basket.

KICK-OUT—A play where the ball-handler waits for the defense to surround him—then quickly passes to a teammate who is open for an outside shot. The ball is not really kicked in this play; the term comes from the action of pinball machines.

NO-LOOK PASS—A play where the passer fools a defender (with his eyes) into covering one teammate—then suddenly passes to another without looking.

PICK-AND-ROLL—A play where one teammate blocks or "picks off" another's defender with his body—then cuts to the basket for a pass in the confusion.

Glossary

BASKETBALL WORDS TO KNOW

ALL-STAR GAME—A game played each year between two teams made up of the league's best players.

ASSISTS—Passes that lead to successful shots.

AVERAGED—Made an average of.

BALL-HANDLER—The person dribbling the basketball.

BOX OUT—Used the body to move an opponent away from the basket with the body.

CLUTCH SHOT—A basket made under pressure.

DEEP—Having a lot of good players.

HALL OF FAME—The place where the game's greatest players are honored; these players are often called "Hall of Famers."

IN THE PAINT—Positioned in the area of the court near the basket, which is usually painted a different color than the rest of the court.

MISMATCHES—Situations in which one player has a great advantage over another.

MOST VALUABLE PLAYER (MVP)—An award given each year to the league's best player; also given to the top player in the league finals and All-Star Game.

NATIONAL BASKETBALL ASSOCIATION (NBA)—The professional league that has been operating since the 1946–47 season.

NBA FINALS—The playoff series which decides the championship of the league.

OVERTIME—The five-minute period played to determine the winner of a tie game.

PLAYOFFS—The games played after the season to determine the league champion.

PRE-SEASON GAME—A practice game against another team.

PROFESSIONAL—A person or team that plays a sport for money. College players are not paid, so they are considered "amateurs."

ROLE PLAYERS—People who are asked to do specific things when they are in a game.

ROOKIE OF THE YEAR—An award given to the league's best first-year player or "rookie."

SEASON TICKETS—A set of tickets for each home game.

UPSET—Beat a much better team.

WESTERN CONFERENCE—One of two groups of teams that make up the NBA. The Western Conference champions play the Eastern Conference champions in the NBA Finals.

OTHER WORDS TO KNOW

BANNED—Kept away or ruled against.

CONTENDER—A person or team good enough to compete for a prize or championship.

DYNAMIC—Full of strength and energy.

EXECUTIVE—A person who makes important decisions in a business.

EXTRAORDINARY—Unusual, or unusually talented.

GENERAL MANAGER—The person responsible for overseeing all business.

INDUCTED—Elected or picked to join a special group.

INGRAINED—Part of someone, like the grain in a piece of wood.

INTIMIDATING—Scaring or threatening.

LOGO—A symbol or design that represents a business or team.

LURE—Attract with the promise of a reward.

MAJESTIC—Grand or splendid.

OVERWHELM—Defeat using much greater force.

SATIN—A smooth, shiny fabric.

SENSATION—The cause of excitement.

SYNTHETIC—Made in a laboratory, not in nature.

TRADITION—A belief or custom that is handed down from generation to generation.

UNSELFISH—Thinking of others first.

Places to Go

ON THE ROAD

AMERICA WEST ARENA
201 East Jefferson Street
Phoenix, Arizona 85004
(602) 379-7900

NAISMITH MEMORIAL BASKETBALL HALL OF FAME
1000 West Columbus Avenue
Springfield, Massachusetts 01105
(877) 4HOOPLA

ON THE WEB

THE NATIONAL BASKETBALL ASSOCIATION   www.nba.com
   • *to learn more about the league's teams, players, and history*

THE PHOENIX SUNS   www.Suns.com
   • *to learn more about the Phoenix Suns*

THE BASKETBALL HALL OF FAME   www.hoophall.com
   • *to learn more about history's greatest players*

ON THE BOOKSHELF

To learn more about the sport of basketball, look for these books at your library or bookstore:

   • Burgan, Michael. *Great Moments in Basketball*. New York, NY.: World Almanac, 2002.

   • Ingram, Scott. *A Basketball All-Star*. Chicago, IL.: Heinemann Library, 2005.

   • Suen, Anastasia. *The Story of Basketball*. New York, NY.: PowerKids Press, 2002.

47

Index

PAGE NUMBERS IN **BOLD** REFER TO ILLUSTRATIONS.

Abdul-Jabbar, Kareem 36, **36**

Adams, Alvan 8, 21, 40, **40**

Ainge, Danny **19**

America West Arena ...**12**, 13, 47

Barkley, Charles ....8, **9**, 17, 18, **19**, 22, **22** , 26, 27, **28**, 35, **35**, 39, 40, **41**, 43

Bloch, Richard 6

Ceballos, Cedric 37, **37**, 40

Chambers, Tom 8, 43, **43**

Colangelo, Bryan 37

Colangelo, Jerry 6, **24**, 25, 35, 37

Counts, Mel **14**

Davis, Walter 8, 21, 40, **40**, 42

Fitzsimmons, Cotton ...25, 40, **41**

Goodrich, Gail 6, **6**, 20

Gorilla 28, **28**, 34

Hawkins, Connie ....**7** , 8, 21, **21**, 36, 38, 43

Heard, Garfield 29

Johnson, Eddie 40

Johnson, Kevin ..8, 22, **22**, 26, 43

Jordan, Michael 8, **9**, 26, **27**

Kidd, Jason 11, 23

MacLeod, John **17**, 25

Majerle, Dan 22, 26, 27, **27**, 39

Marbury, Stephon 11

Marion, Shawn 11, 23, **23**, 43

Manning, Danny 40

McCoy, Al 39, **39**

Nance, Larry 8, 34, 37, 40

Nash, Steve **4**, 11, **15**, 23, **32**, 35, **35**, 37, 38, 40, 42

Outlaw, Bo **4**

Paxson, John 27

Perry, Curtis **17**

Rodgers, Rodney 40

Scott, Charlie 8

Seattle Center Coliseum 30

Silas, Paul 8

Stoudemire, Amare **10**, 11, 23, **23**, **24**, 35, **35**, 39, 40, 43

Van Arsdale, Dick ....6, 20, **20**, 38, 38 , 42

Van Arsdale, Tom 20, **20**

Veterans' Memorial Coliseum 8, 30, **31**

Walton, Bill 30, **30**

Westphal, Paul 8, 21, **21**, 25, 43

The Team

MARK STEWART has written more than 20 books on basketball, and over 100 sports books for kids. He grew up in New York City during the 1960s rooting for the Knicks and Nets, and now takes his two daughters, Mariah and Rachel, to watch them play. Mark comes from a family of writers. His grandfather was Sunday Editor of *The New York Times* and his mother was Articles Editor of *The Ladies Home Journal* and *McCall's*. Mark has profiled hundreds of athletes over the last 20 years. He has also written several books about his native New York, and New Jersey, his home today. Mark is a graduate of Duke University, with a degree in history. He lives with his daughters and wife, Sarah, overlooking Sandy Hook, NJ.

MATT ZEYSING is the resident historian at the Basketball Hall of Fame in Springfield, Massachusetts. His research interests include the origins of the game of basketball, the development of professional basketball in the first half of the twentieth century, and the culture and meaning of basketball in American society.